Ninja Worrier

#1: Tooth Trouble
#2: The King of Show-and-Tell
#3: Homework Hassles
#4: Don't Sit on My Lunch!
#5: Talent Show Scaredy-Pants
#6: Help! A Vampire's Coming!
#7: Yikes! Bikes!
#8: Halloween Fraidy-Cat
#9: Shark Tooth Tale
#10: Super-Secret Valentine
#11: The Pumpkin Elf Mystery
#12: Stop That Hamster!
#13: The One Hundredth Day of School!
#14: Camping Catastrophe!
#15: Thanksgiving Turkey Trouble
#16: Ready, Set, Snow!
#17: Firehouse Fun!
#18: The Perfect Present
#19: The Penguin Problem
#20: Apple Orchard Race
#21: Going Batty
#22: Science Fair Flop
#23: A Very Crazy Christmas
#24: Shark Attack!
#25: Save the Earth!
#26: The Giant Swing
#27: The Reading Race

2nd Grade

#1: Second Grade Rules!
#2: Snow Day Dare
#3: Secret Santa Surprise
#4: Best Prank Ever
#5: Haunted Hayride
#6: Gingerbread Jitters
#7: A Little Bit Lucky
#8: Rock 'n' Roll

Ninja Worrier

by ABBY KLEIN

illustrated by
JOHN McKINLEY

Scholastic Inc.

To Henry and Wyatt,
Two super cool kids!
Love,
A.K.

ISBN 978-1-338-18270-5

10 9 8 7 6 5 4 3 2 1   17 18 19 20 21

Printed in the U.S.A.   40

First printing 2017

Book design by Mary Claire Cruz

CHAPTERS

I have a problem. A really, really big problem. Max is the biggest bully in the whole second grade. Every day when I go out to recess, he won't leave me alone. My friend Josh will stand up to him, but I'm too afraid.

Let me tell you about it.

CHAPTER 1

Show-and-Tell

"Okay, everybody," said my teacher, Miss Clark. "Time for show-and-tell. Please put down the books you were reading and come to the rug."

We all walked over to the rug and sat down except for Max. He ran over and then slid into his spot like a baseball player stealing second base.

"Max, please get up and try that again," said Miss Clark. "I don't want you running and sliding. This is not a baseball field. Sliding like that is not safe. You could slide right into someone."

"That's right," said Chloe. "You almost slid right into me!"

"No I didn't, you little fancy-pants," said Max.

"Yes you did!" said Chloe.

"No I didn't!" Max shouted in her face.

"Yes you did! You came *this* close," Chloe said, holding up two fingers about half an inch apart.

"I wasn't anywhere near you! You're crazy," said Max.

"All right, you two need to stop arguing," said Miss Clark. "Chloe, please come sit over here by me, and Max, please get up and try coming to the rug again. But this time, no sliding."

Max looked at Miss Clark and sighed. He got up slowly and went back to his desk. Then he walked over and sat down on the rug.

"Much better," said Miss Clark. "That time you actually had control of your body. Now I think we're ready to start. Who would like to go first today?"

Jessie and Chloe both raised their hands.

"Me! Me, me, me, me, me!" Chloe sang, waving her hand wildly in front of Miss Clark's face. "I really want to go first. Pleeeeeeease!"

"Chloe, I am not going to choose people who are calling out. Jessie, you had a nice quiet hand. You may go first."

Jessie stood up in front of everyone and pulled a small colorful pouch out of her pocket.

"What's that?" asked Max.

"If you're patient, I'm sure Jessie is going to tell us," said Miss Clark.

"'Patient'?" Josh whispered to me. "I don't think he knows the meaning of that word!"

"That's for sure!" I whispered back.

"This is something my *abuela*, my grandma, gave to me," said Jessie. She reached her hand in the pouch and pulled out four teeny-tiny dolls, each no bigger than her pinkie finger.

"Oooooo!" we all said.

"These are worry dolls," said Jessie.

"What's a worry doll?" said Max.

"You tell these dolls all of your worries," said Jessie, "and they hold your worries, so you don't have to keep thinking about them."

"I need some of those," I whispered to Josh.

"You are definitely a big worrier," said Josh. "That's for sure!"

"Every night, I tell the dolls about any worries I have, so I don't have to think about them when I go to sleep," said Jessie. "Then I put the dolls under my pillow, and they take my worries away during the night. It makes me feel so much better!"

"Where did your grandma get them? I think Freddy needs some of his own," Josh said, laughing.

Jessie laughed, too. "They are actually from

Guatemala. She got them when she went down there to visit. Maybe she can get some for Freddy the next time she goes."

"Thank you so much, Jessie," said Miss Clark. "What a great thing to bring in for show-and-tell. Who would like to go next?"

Once again, Chloe waved her hand wildly and yelled, "Me, me, me, me, me!"

This time Miss Clark didn't say anything. She just stared at her and then called on Josh to go next.

Josh walked over to his cubby and then came back to the front of the room. He was hiding something behind his back.

"He's hiding a karate belt! He's hiding a karate belt!" Max yelled. "I saw it! I saw it!"

"Thanks for ruining my surprise," said Josh.

"That was not a very kind thing to do," said Miss Clark. "Please tell Josh you're sorry."

Max just stared at Josh.

"Now, Max," said Miss Clark. "I haven't got all day!"

"Sorry," Max mumbled.

Josh pulled the belt out from behind his back. "This is my karate belt," he said.

"We know that," said Max.

"Anyway," Josh continued, ignoring Max. "I have been taking karate for two years."

"Two years! Wow!" said Jessie. "You must be really good!"

"Can you show us some of your moves?" said Miss Clark.

"Sure," said Josh.

"Everybody, scoot back," said Miss Clark. "Give Josh some room."

We all moved toward the back of the rug.

"Let's see," said Josh. "I'll show you a roundhouse kick first." He stood perfectly still and then all of a sudden he lifted his leg and whipped it around really fast. It was like a blur.

"That was so cool!" said Jessie.

"Would you like to show us something else?" asked Miss Clark.

"I'll show you an upper rising block," said

Josh. "You might want to use it if someone is about to kick you in the face." He lowered his body a little bit, lifted his left fist in front of his face, and pulled his right arm next to his waist.

"Very impressive," said Miss Clark.

"No big deal," Max mumbled. "Anyone can do that."

"That's not true," said Miss Clark. "It takes a lot of practice. Josh told us he's been working on his karate skills for two years."

"Why is your belt orange?" said Chloe. "If I were doing karate, I would choose a pink belt because pink is my favorite color."

"In karate, there are no pink belts," said Josh.

"There aren't?" said Chloe, sticking out her lower lip in a pout.

"No, and besides, you don't get to pick your belt color."

"You don't?" said Chloe. "I don't get it. Why not?"

"Because each time you move up a level, you get a new color belt," said Josh. "The color of your belt shows how advanced you are."

"How many belts do you have?" Jessie asked.

"This is only my third belt," said Josh. "I have a white, a yellow, and now an orange, but one day I want to earn my black belt."

"Black belts are like the guys you see in the movies," said Jessie.

"They have really awesome moves," I said. "They're like ninja warriors."

"Thank you, Josh," said Miss Clark. "It looks like it's almost time for recess."

Chloe stood up and walked to the front of the room.

"What are you doing?" asked Miss Clark.

"My show-and-tell," said Chloe.

"We don't have time for that now," said Miss Clark. "I didn't call on you today because you did not listen to what I said. If you would like a turn tomorrow, then you'll raise your hand quietly and wait patiently."

"But . . . but . . . that's not fair!" Chloe whined.

"Oh, it's very fair," said Miss Clark. "Now, as soon as you all put your books away from quiet reading, you may walk out to recess."

CHAPTER 2

Secret Ninja Warriors

Max grabbed his books, stuffed them in his book bag, and ran over to the bookshelf. "Move!" he said, shoving Chloe out of his way.

Chloe fell on the ground, and her books went flying out of her book bag. "OW! OW! OOOWWWW!" she wailed. "Look what you made me do, you big meanie."

Max ignored her and started running toward the door.

Miss Clark jumped in front of him. "Whoa!

Hold on there, Max," she said, holding her hand up to stop him.

Chloe continued bawling. "He hurt me! He hurt me! I think my wrist is broken."

"Her wrist is broken?" said Jessie. "I don't think so. She is such a drama queen."

"Seriously," whispered Josh. "I really don't think her wrist is broken, but maybe her butt is."

Jessie and I had to cover our mouths so Miss Clark wouldn't see us giggling.

"Where are you going, Max?" asked Miss Clark.

"I was going out to recess," he said.

"I don't think so," said Miss Clark.

"But didn't you just say it was time for recess?"

"Yes, I did," said Miss Clark. "But I also said to walk, and I never said to shove someone out of your way. Look what happened to poor Chloe. I think you need to help her."

Max just stared at Chloe, but he didn't move.

"I don't think he knows the meaning of the word 'help,' " Jessie whispered.

"Max," said Miss Clark. "You are not going out to recess until you apologize to Chloe and help her pick up the books that went flying out of her bag when you shoved her."

"Apologize to Chloe. That might take until lunchtime," Josh said, laughing.

"I know," I said. "Let's get going. Maybe this will be one recess where I can actually have fun without Max bothering me."

We dashed out the door. "Beat you to the big tree!" yelled Josh.

"Hey, Josh, wait for me!" I yelled as I ran across the playground after him.

"Hurry up, Freddy," Josh called over his shoulder. "Robbie is already there waiting for us."

My other best friend, Robbie, was standing by the big tree. We meet him there every day at recess, so we can all play together.

When I finally reached the tree, I stood there panting for a second. "Wow, Josh, you sure are

fast," I said. "I thought Jessie was a fast runner, but you're pretty speedy, too!"

Josh smiled and pointed to the ground. "I think it's these new shoes I just got yesterday."

"Those are cool," said Robbie. "Where did you get them? Maybe I need to get a pair if they make you run like a superhero."

Josh laughed. "I just got them at that place

in the mall. The guy in the store told me they were the fastest shoes he had."

"Well, he was right," said Robbie. "They practically make you fly!"

"Should we play superheroes today?" asked Josh. "I could be The Flash."

"Nah," I said. "I feel like playing something else."

"What should we play?" asked Robbie.

"Have you guys seen that new show on television called *Secret Ninja Spies*?" Josh asked.

"Oh yeah! I love that show!" said Robbie.

"Me, too!" I said. "I was just watching it last night."

"Those guys have the coolest moves," said Josh, karate-chopping and kicking the air.

"They always have a secret mission," said Robbie. "They have to track someone down and rescue that person from the bad guys."

"Who should we track? Who should we pretend to rescue?" I said.

"I know!" said Robbie. "Let's rescue Jessie.

She's always a good sport. She'll play along. Where is she now?" He scanned the playground.

I looked around, too. "I don't see her."

"You know who else I don't see," said Robbie. "I don't see Max."

"That's because he's still in the classroom," I said.

"Why?" said Robbie.

"Max pushed Chloe down right when it was time to go out. Miss Clark is making him apologize to her."

Robbie laughed. "That might take until lunchtime!" he said.

"That's exactly what I said," answered Josh.

"So for once we can play without him bothering us," I said.

"Oh! I see Jessie! There she is!" said Josh.

"Where?" asked Robbie. "I don't see her anywhere."

"Over there by the soccer field," Josh said, pointing his finger in that direction.

"We have to move slowly and quietly so she doesn't hear us coming," said Robbie.

"And if any bad guys get in our way, we will karate-chop them," said Josh.

"Ninjas, ready?" said Robbie.

"Ready!" we all said together.

The three of us took off running across the playground. "Watch out! Hot lava!" Robbie yelled, and we jumped over the sandbox.

"A bomb! A bomb!" Josh screamed, and we ducked under a basketball that was flying through the air.

As we got closer to the soccer field, we hid behind a tree. "What now, ninjas?" Robbie whispered.

"We just have to use our black-belt karate skills to make our way through that wall of bad guys," I said, pointing to the other kids on the soccer field, "and then we can rescue Jessie."

Then I heard it. That laugh. I would know it anywhere.

"Ha, ha, ha! Black-belt karate skills! That's the funniest thing I've ever heard," Max said.

"Why is that so funny?" said Josh.

"Because Freddy couldn't hurt a fly even if he tried," said Max.

"I thought he wasn't coming out to recess," whispered Robbie.

"I wish he'd leave us alone just once," I whispered back. "Just leave us alone."

I must have said that a little louder than I thought because Max grabbed the collar of my shirt and pulled me right up to his face. "What did you say, little baby?" I could feel his hot, stinky breath sting my eyes.

I gulped.

"He said 'leave us alone,'" said Josh. "Now, let go of Freddy's shirt."

Max spun around. "Wanna make me, little ninja?" he said, raising his fist to Josh's face.

Before Max knew what was happening, Josh did three quick karate moves, and Max was lying on the ground, looking up at us.

“Come on, ninjas. Let’s go,” Josh said with a big smile on his face.

I just stood there frozen, looking down at Max. I couldn’t believe my eyes. In three swift moves, Josh had taken down the biggest bully in the whole second grade. I decided right then and there that I was going to have to learn some real karate!

CHAPTER 3

Mashed Potato Ninja

On the bus ride home, Robbie and I could not stop talking about Josh's takedown of Max.

"You were amazing at recess today!" Robbie said to Josh.

"That was one of the most awesome things I've ever seen!" I said.

Jessie leaned over her seat. "What are you guys talking about? What did Josh do?"

"You should have seen it, Jessie," I said. "You would have been really impressed."

"Seen what? What happened?"

"Freddy, Josh, and I were playing ninjas, and

then Josh turned into a real live ninja!" said Robbie.

"One minute Max was standing up holding my shirt, and then I blinked, and he was down on the ground!" I said.

"Really?" said Jessie.

"Really!" I said. "Max didn't even know what hit him!"

"I wish I had been there to see that," said Jessie. "That must have been great!"

"It was!" I said. "It really was!"

"Did Max get hurt?" asked Jessie.

"No," said Josh. "I didn't want to hurt him. I just wanted to get him off of Freddy. Karate is only supposed to be used for self-defense. I just basically flipped him onto the ground."

"Did you learn those moves in your karate class?" Jessie asked Josh.

"Yes. I started karate out in California, and I just found a new dojo here, so I started taking classes again."

"Is it hard?" I asked.

"It's not easy, but it's really fun," said Josh.

"How long have you been doing karate?" asked Robbie.

"About two years," said Josh.

"Two years! No wonder you're so good," Robbie said. "What color belt are you?"

"I'm only an orange belt right now," said Josh, "but someday I want to be a black belt."

"Being a black belt would be so cool!" I said.

"You should take karate classes," said Josh. "Then Max just might stop bullying you."

"That's a great idea," said Jessie. "You should do karate, Freddy."

"I don't know . . ."

"You don't know what?" said Jessie.

"I don't know if I'd be very good at it."

"You'll never know unless you try," said Josh.

I thought about that awesome takedown again. "Maybe I will," I said, smiling. "Maybe I will."

That night at dinner my sister, Suzie, was going on and on about her latest spelling test. "The words were really hard this week. I had to study a lot. I wasn't sure how I was going to do, but I got the best grade in the whole class!" she bragged. "Isn't that great?"

"Whoop-de-doo," I muttered under my breath.

"That is great, honey," said my mom.

"I'm really proud of you," said my dad. "Like I always say, 'practice makes perfect.'"

Enough about Suzie, I thought to myself. I tapped my spoon on the edge of my plate, cleared my throat, and said, "I have an announcement to make."

"Oh, really?" said Suzie, snickering. "What's the announcement? That you just peed in your pants?"

I turned and glared at her. "Ha, ha! Very funny. No, I did not just pee in my pants."

"Suzie!" said my mom. "That is not funny at all. That is very rude. I'm sure Freddy has something very exciting to tell us."

"I do." I cleared my throat again. "Uhhmmm. I am going to take karate lessons."

Suzie burst out laughing. "You!" she said, pointing her finger at me. "*You* are going to take karate lessons?"

"Why is that so funny?" I said.

"Because you are such a fraidy-cat! You are even afraid of your own shadow."

"No I'm not."

"Yes you are."

"No I'm not."

"Oh, yes you are!"

"All right. That's enough, you two," said my

dad. "I think it's a great idea for you to take karate, Freddy."

"You do?"

"Yes, I do. It's good to learn how to defend yourself. You don't use karate to hurt other people. You use it for self-defense."

"That's exactly what Josh said today. You know, he takes karate."

"He does?" said my mom.

"Yeah. He's been taking karate for two years, and he's an orange belt now. You should have seen what he did today at recess!" I said.

"What did he do?" asked my dad.

"Max was holding me by my shirt collar," I said. "Then out of nowhere, Josh does three quick moves, and Max is lying on the ground. It looked like this." I stood up to demonstrate—karate-chopped my hands wildly in the air and spun around.

"Freddy, watch what you're doing . . . ," my mom started to say, but it was too late. I accidentally knocked into my dinner plate, sending peas and mashed potatoes flying through the air. A big plop of mashed potatoes landed in my hair.

"Ha, ha, ha, ha, ha!" Suzie laughed hysterically. "Those are some real ninja-like moves you've got there. Smooth . . . real smooth."

Some of the mashed potatoes were starting to drip off the ends of my hair, and I stuck out my tongue to catch them in my mouth.

"Ewww! That's gross," said Suzie. "Did you just eat potatoes that dripped out of your hair?"

"Freddy!" said my mom. "Stop that! Let me get a dish towel, so I can wipe the food out of your hair." She went over to the sink and wet the dish towel a little bit. Then she came back to the table. "Now, stand still. I need to clean you off. There. I think I got most of it, but you're still going to have to take a shower and wash your hair tonight."

"Awww, Mom. Do I really have to? I think it's clean enough."

"No it's not, mister, and you're not going to school with dried-up crusty potatoes in your hair."

"But *Secret Ninja Spies* is on in half an hour, and I really need to watch it."

"Well, you should have thought of that before you karate-chopped your dinner."

"If I go shower now, I might just make it in time to watch. May I be excused?" I said.

"Are you finished eating?" asked my dad.

"I don't think my hair is hungry anymore," I said, laughing.

"Clear your plate and pick up the peas off the floor," said my mom. "Then you may be excused."

I cleaned up my dinner mess, and then I kicked and punched my way up the stairs to the bathroom.

CHAPTER 4

Ninja Cooties

I ran into the bathroom and shut the door. I didn't need Suzie bugging me while I was taking a shower. I turned on the water, took off my clothes, and jumped in. I didn't have time to waste if I was going to make it back downstairs in time for the start of *Secret Ninja Spies*.

I lathered up my hair with shampoo and started singing. "Watch out, here they come . . . Secret Ninja Spies . . . ooo, ooo, ooo."

Just then the bathroom door flung open. "Where's the sick cat?" Suzie asked frantically.

"Get out! Get out!" I shouted.

"I heard this awful noise, so I came as quickly as I could to help the poor sick cat."

"There is no sick cat in here!" I yelled. "Get out of here now!"

"But I heard this terrible screeching sound."

"Very funny," I said. "That was me singing."

"That was you singing? It sounded like a sick cat. All right, then. I'll leave now," said Suzie, slamming the door on her way out.

Sometimes I wished I had a brother instead of a sister.

I rinsed out my hair and quickly soaped up my body. I tried one of the karate kicks I saw Josh use today, but lost my balance and almost slipped and fell. Karate in the shower was probably not such a good idea!

I washed off the soap and checked one last time to make sure there was no more dried potato in my hair. I knew my mom was going to check when I got out of the shower, and if there was still potato in my hair, she'd make me get back in. I didn't have time for that. I got out of the shower, and as I was drying myself off, Suzie barged into the bathroom again.

"Hey! How about a little privacy?" I said.

Suzie ignored me and started putting toothpaste on her toothbrush.

"What are you doing?" I asked.

"What does it look like I'm doing, Sharkbreath?" said Suzie. "Making a cake?"

She brought the toothbrush up to her lips and was about to put it in her mouth when I grabbed it out of her hand.

"Hey! Give me that back," she said, reaching for the toothbrush.

"You can have it back when I'm done in the bathroom," I said.

"No, you'll give it to me now," said Suzie.

"Oh, no I won't," I said, hiding the toothbrush behind my back.

"Oh, yes you will. I don't have time for your silly games, Freddy," said Suzie. "*Anna Banana* is on in ten minutes."

"*Anna Banana*. That is such a dumb show," I said. "I can't believe you even watch that."

"It's the best show on TV," said Suzie.

"*Secret Ninja Spies* is the best show on TV," I said.

"Now, *that* is a really dumb show," said Suzie, rolling her eyes.

"No it's not," I said. "Besides, it's my turn to choose the show we watch, and I'm not watching *Anna Banana*. I'm watching *Secret Ninja Spies* tonight."

"It is not your turn to choose," said Suzie.

"Yes it is. It's Tuesday, and on Tuesdays I get to choose what we watch," I said, hugging my towel a little more tightly around myself.

"For your information," said Suzie with her hands on her hips, "it's not Tuesday. It's Wednesday, and Wednesdays are *my* day to choose what we watch."

"Wednesday?" I said. "Are you sure?"

"Of course I'm sure," said Suzie. "I had ballet today, and I always have ballet on Wednesdays."

"But I have to watch *Secret Ninja Spies* tonight," I whined. "I promised Josh and Robbie I would, so we could play tomorrow at recess."

"Oh well. Too bad for you," said Suzie.

"Come on, Suzie," I begged. "Let me just watch it tonight."

"Okay," said Suzie.

Okay? Did she just say "okay"?

"What's it worth to you?" Suzie asked, holding up her pinkie for a pinkie swear.

I knew there was a catch. I knew it wouldn't be that easy!

"How about you can have double computer time tomorrow?"

"Tomorrow? Just tomorrow?" Suzie snickered. "You'll have to do better than that."

"Are you kidding?" I said.

"No I'm not," said Suzie. "And we're running out of time, so if you don't hurry up, then there'll be no deal."

"Fine. You can have double computer time

for the next three days," I said, holding up my pinkie. "Do we have a deal?"

"Yes we do," said Suzie, smiling, as she locked her pinkie with mine. "We have a deal. Now can I have my toothbrush back?"

I looked down at my hand holding her toothbrush. I forgot I was still holding it. Some of the toothpaste was starting to slide off, so I licked it.

"Ewwww! That is so gross!" said Suzie. "You just licked my toothbrush."

"So? What's the big deal?" I said.

"What's the big deal?" said Suzie. "The big deal is that you have cooties, and you just put them on my toothbrush."

I laughed and licked her toothbrush again. "There, now you have ninja cooties on your toothbrush."

Suzie tried to grab the toothbrush out of my hand. "Give that to me!" she said. "I have to clean it off before I use it."

"Fine. Fine. Here you go," I said, handing her the toothbrush. I realized that my show was about to start any minute, and I needed to get my pajamas on fast.

I looked on the floor of the bathroom where I usually leave my pajamas in the morning, but I didn't see them.

"Suzie, did you take my pajamas?" I asked.

"Nuh-uh," Suzie mumbled, her mouth full of toothpaste.

Maybe my mom picked them up and put them in the dirty-clothes hamper. She is such a neat freak. She doesn't like anything lying on the floor.

I bent over the hamper and started tossing dirty clothes out into the bathroom . . . a pair of pants, a T-shirt, one dirty sock, then another.

"Ahhh!" screamed Suzie.

I turned around and saw that one of my dirty socks had landed on her head and was hanging down right in front of her nose.

I burst out laughing. "Ha, ha, ha, ha, ha!"

Suzie shook her head, and the sock flew off and landed on the floor. She spit out her toothpaste. "That sock is disgusting! It smells like poop. I'm getting out of here," she said, and ran out the door.

That's one way to get rid of her, I thought to myself. *I'll have to remember that for some other time when she's bugging me.*

I dug around in the hamper some more and finally found my favorite hammerhead shark pajamas. I threw them on, dried my head quickly with my towel, and ran my fingers through my hair. No time for a brush.

"Mom!" I shouted. "What time is it?"

"It's 7:59!" she yelled from downstairs.

Holy cow, it's 7:59? I only had one more minute before the show started. I had to be quick like a ninja. I bounded down the stairs two at a time, pretending every other step was quicksand that I had to avoid, and landed on the couch just in time for the show to start.

CHAPTER 5

Lunch Ninja

The next day at lunch, Josh started talking about *Secret Ninja Spies*.

"Did you guys see last night's episode?" he said.

"Of course I did," said Robbie. "I wouldn't miss it!"

"How about you, Freddy? Did you see it?" asked Josh.

"I almost missed it."

"Really? Why?" said Robbie.

"It was Suzie's night to pick what we watched on TV, and she wanted to watch *Anna Banana*."

"*Anna Banana*? What's that?" asked Josh.

"A really dumb show," said Robbie. "My sister, Kimberly, loves that show, too."

"So how did you convince her to watch *Secret Ninja Spies*?" said Josh.

"Let me guess," said Robbie. "It cost you something."

I nodded. "Yep. Suzie gets double computer time for the next three days!"

"Wow!" said Josh. "I'm glad I don't have a big sister."

"It was worth it, though, because that was one of the best episodes ever!" I said.

"I know," said Josh. "Those ninjas have some serious moves!"

"I thought it was so cool when that one guy did the spinning kick and knocked out three bad guys at once!" Robbie said.

"Josh, do you know how to do that kind of kick?" I asked.

"Not yet," said Josh. "That's pretty advanced."

"What kind of kicks have you learned?" asked Robbie.

Freddy

"Let's see . . . I can do a roundhouse kick, a side kick, a front kick, and a back kick," said Josh.

"Wow! That's a lot," said Robbie.

"You could learn those kicks, too," said Josh. "Why don't you take karate lessons?"

"Guess what?" I said.

"What?" said Josh.

"I told my parents that you take karate lessons, and they said that I could take lessons, too!"

Just then Max butted into the conversation. "What kind of lessons are you going to take, little baby? Ballet lessons?"

"I take ballet lessons!" said Chloe. "They are so much fun! Watch what I can do." She jumped up off the bench and started spinning around the cafeteria.

"No one cares!" yelled Max.

Chloe ignored him. "I can do three pirouettes in a row," she said.

"What did she just say?" I asked Robbie. "A pir-o-what?"

"A pirouette. That's a fancy word for a spin on your toes," Robbie explained.

"Here I go," said Chloe. "You can count them. One, two—"

She was about to do the third one, but Max stuck out his foot and tripped her. Chloe crashed to the floor.

"OW! OW! OW!" she wailed. "Someone help me!"

The lunch teacher came running over. "Chloe, what happened? Are you all right?"

"No! I'm not all right," she sniffled. "Max tripped me while I was showing everybody my pirouettes."

"I didn't trip you," said Max. "You just fell on your butt."

"I did not!" said Chloe.

"Yes you did," said Max.

"Stop arguing, you two," said the lunch teacher. She reached out her hand to Chloe. "Here—let me help you up."

Chloe stood up. "I think I need to go to the nurse to get some ice for my ankle," she said. "I think I sprained it."

"Sprained it?" Robbie whispered. "She looks like she's standing on it just fine."

"She'll do anything for attention," said Josh. "Watch, she'll start limping now."

Sure enough, Chloe limped out the cafeteria door to the nurse's office.

"Max, you need to take your lunch and go sit over there by yourself," said the lunch teacher, "and think about what you've done."

Max grabbed his lunch and sulked off to the corner table.

"Well, at least we can now eat our lunch without him bothering us," said Robbie.

"It is a lot quieter without his big blabbering mouth," said Josh.

"Did you say that you are going to take karate lessons?" said Jessie.

"Yes! Last night I told my parents all about

Josh's takedown of Max yesterday, and they were really impressed," I said.

Josh smiled.

"I tried to show them, but I accidentally karate-chopped my plate and got mashed potatoes in my hair."

"Ha, ha!" Robbie laughed. "I wish I had been there to see that!"

"So when do you get to start?" asked Josh.

"Today!" I said. "I can't wait. My mom is going to take me to the dojo after school."

"Did you get your *gi* yet?" asked Josh.

"My what?"

"Your *gi*. That's the name of your karate uniform. You know—the white shirt and pants that people wear when they do karate."

"Oh! I didn't know it had a name," I said, laughing. "My mom is getting it for me today while I'm at school, so I'll have it for this afternoon."

"What about the belt?" said Robbie.

"The sensei will give it to him when he goes to his first class," said Josh.

"The who?" I said.

"The sensei. That's what you call a karate teacher," said Josh.

"Boy! I have a lot to learn," I said.

"What color belt do you start with?" asked Jessie.

"Everyone starts with a white belt," said Josh. "That's the beginner level. Then after that you get a yellow one."

"Anything else you think I need to know before I go?" I asked Josh.

"Just make sure you always stay focused and stand up straight with your hands by your sides when the sensei is talking or demonstrating something."

I jumped off the bench. "Like this?" I said, standing up nice and tall and straight like a soldier.

"Perfect!" said Josh. "And never talk when the sensei is talking."

"I will keep my lips zipped," I said, pretending to zip my lips closed.

"Karate is about focus, discipline, and respect," said Josh.

"It sounds like a lot of fun," said Jessie.

"You should try it, too," I said. "I bet you would be really good at it."

"You know, karate isn't just for boys," said Josh. "There are lots of girls in my class."

"Maybe I'll try it sometime," said Jessie.

"I am so excited! I can't wait!" I said, and karate-chopped my sandwich. But instead of cutting it in half, I just smushed it and tuna fish squished out all over the table.

"Hey, ninja Freddy, why don't you save your warrior moves for the dojo," Josh said, laughing.

CHAPTER 6

Karate Class

I couldn't wait for school to be over so I could go to karate class. I was so excited.

"Good luck! Have fun!" Josh yelled as I jumped off the bus.

"Thanks!" I shouted over my shoulder. "I will!"

I threw open the front door and yelled, "Mom, I'm home! Where are you? Where's my *gi*?"

"I'm in here, Freddy," my mom called from the kitchen.

I raced into the kitchen. "Hey, Mom, where's my *gi*?"

"Your what?" said my mom.

"My *gi*."

"What's that?"

I laughed. "Josh told me that's the real name of a karate uniform. Did you get it? Did you get it?" I asked, jumping up and down.

"Yes, I did. It's right here," said my mom as she pulled it out of the bag. "I hope it fits."

I yanked off my shirt and pants to try on my uniform just as Suzie came walking into the kitchen.

"Nice undies," Suzie said, laughing. "What's going on?"

"I have my first karate class today."

"And you're going in your underwear?" said Suzie.

"No, I'm not going in my underwear," I said. "I'm trying on the uniform Mom bought for me today."

I put the *gi* shirt over my head and pulled up the pants. "Perfect!" I said.

"Aren't you missing something?" said Suzie.

"What?"

"The belt! Don't you need one of those black belts?"

"A black belt! You don't start with a black belt!" I said.

"Well, excuse me," said Suzie. "Whenever I see karate guys on TV, they always have black belts on."

"That's because they're experts. Beginners start with a white belt."

"So, where's your white belt?" asked Suzie.

"Josh said that the sensei gives it to you at your first class."

"The who?" said Suzie.

"The sensei. That's the Japanese word for 'karate teacher,' " I said.

"Well, have fun. I'm going over to Kimberly's house. *Sayonara*—that's Japanese for 'good-bye,' " Suzie said, and she walked out.

"Freddy, we'd better get going," said my mom. "We don't want to be late. Let's go."

We jumped in the car, and my mom drove

me to the dojo. I started getting a little nervous on the ride over.

"What if this is really hard?" I said. "What if I can't do the moves?"

"Oh, you'll be fine, Freddy. Stop worrying," said my mom.

"But I don't want to embarrass myself. I don't want people to laugh at me."

"No one is going to laugh at you," said my mom. "Just have fun."

When we got there, I ran inside and froze. "There are a lot of kids here," I whispered to my mom. "And they all look like they know what they're doing."

"They're all beginners just like you," my mom whispered back.

Just then a man wearing a black belt came up to me. "Hello. You must be Freddy. I'm sensei Ryan. Nice to meet you," he said, and bowed in my direction.

"Nice to meet you, too," I said.

"In Japan, if someone bows to you," said

Ryan, "then you bow back. It's how we greet each other."

"Oh! Sorry!" I said, bowing.

"Here is your belt," said Ryan. "Why don't you put it on and come join us."

My mom helped me tie my belt. Now I felt like a real ninja warrior!

"Remember, have fun!" my mom whispered.

I went to join the other kids on the mats. *"Konnichiwa,"* said Ryan. "Hello, everybody. I'd like to introduce you to Freddy. He's going to be joining our class."

"Konnichiwa, Freddy," everyone said, and then bowed toward me.

I bowed back.

"Today we are going to be working on some basic punches, blocks, and kicks," said Ryan.

I smiled. *This is going to be so cool,* I thought to myself.

"Freddy, do you know why we learn karate?" asked Ryan.

"To protect ourselves?" I said.

"That's right," said Ryan. "We don't pick fights with people. We use our karate skills to protect ourselves if someone comes after us."

"Like Max," I mumbled to myself.

"First, let's try a side kick. Remember—you want to hit with the blade of your foot and keep your toes pointing down. Like this," Ryan said, demonstrating a side kick. "Now it's your turn to try."

I lifted my right leg and tried to copy exactly what Ryan had done, but my leg just sort of wiggled out to the side.

"Freddy, try again, but this time bring your knee up first, then extend your leg, and then bring it back in before you put it down. It's on four counts . . . up, out, in, down. Watch me." Ryan did it again, slowly counting. "One, two, three, four. Now you try."

I tried again, and this time my leg didn't wiggle around so much.

"Great! You're starting to get it. Try again, but remember you want to show strength. Really extend your leg with force."

I counted silently in my head as I thrust my leg out to the side.

"Much better!" said Ryan. "Now you're getting the hang of it."

We did ten side kicks on the right side and then ten on the left.

"In karate there is a lot of repetition," said Ryan. "That's how you improve your skills. You practice over, and over, and over."

I heard my dad's voice in my head, *practice makes perfect.*

"Now let's try a forward punch," said Ryan. "Stand with your right leg slightly in front of your left, like this. We call this front stance."

I copied exactly what he did.

"Freddy, you don't want to stand up perfectly straight. Bend your knees a bit and get a little lower, so you feel like a sturdy tree with your roots going deep into the ground and nothing can knock you over."

I bent my knees a little bit and moved my feet a little farther apart.

"Now, when you punch, you want to make sure that you hit with the first two knuckles of your right hand, and you want to pull your left fist back to your waist. Watch me." Ryan demonstrated slowly. "Now you all try it."

The whole class tried a forward punch.

"You want to make sure you have power in your punch. Pulling that other fist back to your waist at the same time you extend your front arm helps make your punch stronger. Try again."

We tried again.

"In order to have the greatest impact in karate, you need to release your stored energy. You do this by shouting or yelling when you strike. When you punch, you want to yell *'Ki-ai!'* Let's try that."

We all punched and yelled, *"Ki-ai!"*

"Great! Do it again, but louder this time."

"Ki-ai!" we all shouted.

"That was awesome!" said Ryan. "Could you feel the power?"

I felt powerful, all right, but was I powerful enough to stand up to Max?

CHAPTER 7

Cereal Side Kick

I practiced what I had learned in karate class before I went to bed, and I got up early the next morning to practice again.

"Ki-ai! Ki-ai!" I shouted as I punched the air.

Suzie barged into my room.

"Get out!" I yelled. "If the door is closed, you're supposed to knock."

"What are you doing, weirdo?" said Suzie.

"I'm practicing karate. Now, leave me alone."

"Well, Mom says you need to come down for breakfast."

"I'll be there in a minute," I said as I shoved

GREAT

her out the door. If I was ever going to be able to stand up to Max Sellars, then I'd have to practice a lot!

A few minutes later, I heard my mom calling from downstairs, "Freddy! Freddy! Where are you?"

"I'm in my room!" I yelled back.

"Well, you need to get down here right now and eat your breakfast, or you're going to miss the bus."

I glanced at the clock. Oh no, 7:15! I was so focused on karate that I had completely lost track of time!

I bounded down the stairs and raced into the kitchen.

Suzie was pointing at me and laughing hysterically.

"What's so funny?" I said.

"You . . . you . . . you . . ." She was laughing so hard she couldn't get the words out.

"What?" I demanded.

"Did you forget something?" she said.

"No, I didn't forget anything."

"So you're planning on going to school like that?"

"Like what?" I looked down. I wasn't wearing any pants! I had taken my pants off when I was practicing my karate kicks because my foot kept getting caught in the pant leg. I forgot to put them back on before I came downstairs.

"I'm sure your friends would love to see your tighty whities," said Suzie. "They are so cute with the sharks all over them."

My face turned bright red. I could feel my cheeks burning.

"Freddy, you are already running late," said my mom. "Go back upstairs and put on some pants. You need to hurry!"

I ran upstairs, threw on my pants, and dashed back into the kitchen.

"Much better," said my mom. "Now, what would you like for breakfast? You haven't got a lot of time."

"I'll just have a bowl of cereal," I said.

My mom brought me the box of cereal and some milk. "Here you go," she said. "Eat up."

"Thanks, Mom," I said, pouring the cereal into my bowl.

"Freddy, why are you so late this morning?" asked my dad. "I thought I heard a noise in your room really early this morning. Earlier than usual."

"He thinks he's a ninja," said Suzie.

I glared at her. "I did get up early, Dad, because I wanted to practice karate before I went to school."

"Really?" said my dad. "I guess you really liked your class yesterday."

"It was awesome! We were learning punches, and kicks, and blocks."

"You were learning all of that in your first class?"

"Yep. You want to see?" I said, jumping up from the table.

"Freddy, I don't think . . . ," my mom started to say, but before she could stop me, I did a side kick, and my foot landed right in my cereal bowl. The bowl flipped upside down and milk spilled all over the floor.

"Freddy!" said my mom. "Look what you just did!"

I stood there in my sopping-wet sock, watching the milk form a puddle on the kitchen floor.

"The kitchen is not a place to do karate."

"Sorry, Mom."

"Now go get a sponge and clean up this mess!"

I ran over to the sink, got a sponge, and wiped up the floor. Now both of my socks were soaking wet and squishy.

"Give me your socks and go upstairs and get some dry ones," said my mom. "You'll just have to take a bagel with you on the bus."

I got back downstairs just as the bus pulled up. I grabbed my backpack and a bagel and ran out the door.

When I got on the bus, I was so excited to

tell Robbie and Josh about my karate class that I didn't see Max stick his leg out when I was walking down the aisle. I tripped right over his foot, fell on the floor, and dropped my bagel. I tried to grab it, but it rolled out of my reach under a seat.

"There goes my breakfast," I sighed.

When I looked up, Max had a big grin on his face. "Are you okay, Freddy? Did you trip?"

"Big bully," I muttered under my breath.

Max bent down low, so the bus driver couldn't see, and grabbed my shirt collar. "What did you say?" he growled in my face.

"Nothing. I didn't say anything," I mumbled.

"Freddy," said the bus driver. "Would you please get up and take your seat? I can't start driving until you sit down."

Max slowly let go of my shirt. I stood up, brushed myself off, and walked to the back of the bus.

"Freddy, are you okay?" asked Robbie.

"What happened?" asked Josh.

"Max tripped me," I said.

"I don't know why he doesn't just leave you alone," said Robbie.

"He will soon," said Josh. "Now that you're taking karate. How was class yesterday?"

"It was awesome!" I said.

"Really?" said Robbie. "What kind of stuff did you learn?"

"I learned how to do a side kick."

"That's cool," said Robbie.

"It was a little hard at first," I said. "My leg was wiggling around like a worm, but I think I'm getting the hang of it."

"It just takes practice, that's all," said Josh. "The side kick is one of the hardest."

"What else did you learn?" said Robbie.

"Let's see . . . we practiced a forward punch. You punch with your right hand, and your left hand comes back to your side."

"Your hands move in opposite directions of each other," said Josh. "That way you have more power. Did your sensei teach you about the karate yell?"

"The karate yell? What's that?" asked Robbie.

"When you punch, you yell *ki-ai* to let out your stored energy. It makes your punch stronger," said Josh. "It sounds like this." Josh punched the air and yelled, *"Ki-ai!"*

"Wow!" said Robbie. "That is like real ninja warrior stuff! Can you guys show me some of that?"

"Sure!" said Josh.

"Why don't we all practice some karate at recess?" said Robbie.

"Great idea!" said Josh.

I put my finger to my lips. "SHHHH!" I said. "I don't want you-know-who to even know I'm taking karate. I just want to surprise him one day."

"It will be a surprise, all right," Josh whispered. "A real surprise!"

CHAPTER 8

The Surprise

As I was walking into the classroom, Max smiled, patted me on the back, and said, "Freddy, did you have a nice trip?"

"Oh, Freddy, I didn't know you were going on a trip," said Miss Clark. "Where did you go?"

I glared at Max, and then I turned to Miss Clark. "He was just joking. I didn't go on a trip," I said.

"He just thinks he's so funny," whispered Josh.

"I know," I said. "But he's not. He's just mean."

We all put our stuff away in our cubbies and sat down to work. It was hard for me to concentrate because I couldn't stop thinking about practicing karate with Josh and Robbie at recess. The morning seemed to go by really slowly, even slower than usual.

Finally, Miss Clark said, "It's just about time for recess. Please put your books away, and then you can go out."

We all walked over to put our books away, but Max was in such a hurry that he bumped into the bookshelf, and two baskets of books toppled onto the floor.

"Who just did that?" asked Miss Clark.

Before I could think about what I was saying, the words came flying out of my mouth. "Max did it," I said.

Max whipped his head around and glared at me. I gulped.

"Max, you really need to slow down and control your body," said Miss Clark. "You are not going out to recess until all of these books are cleaned up."

"You're in big trouble now," Max whispered in my ear. "Just wait until I get out to recess."

I grabbed Josh by the arm. "Come on! Let's get out of here!"

I didn't stop running until we were out on the playground. "Freddy, are you okay?" asked Robbie. "You look a little weird."

"Max just whispered something to him," said Josh.

"What did he say?" asked Robbie.

"He said he was going to get me at recess," I said.

"Whatever!" said Josh. "Don't even think about him. Let's just go have some fun."

"Yeah," said Robbie. "I want you guys to show me some real karate moves."

"I want to find a secret place to practice," I said.

"You mean because we're Secret Ninja Spies, so we need a secret hangout," said Josh.

"No, because I don't want Max to find me," I said. "I don't know what he's going to do!"

"You're getting yourself all worried for nothing," said Josh, "but if it will make you feel better, we can find a secret place to practice."

"We could go to the far end of the field, behind that row of trees," said Robbie.

"No, anyone can see us there," I said. "The trees are too skinny."

"What about under the slide?" said Josh.

"There's not enough room to practice kicking and punching there," said Robbie.

"I know!" I said. "Follow me."

Josh and Robbie followed me around the side of the building and behind the ball shed. "No one will find us here," I said, smiling.

"Good thinking," said Josh. "I've never been back here."

"Can you guys show me how to do some real karate?" asked Robbie.

"Sure," said Josh. "Let's try a forward punch. "Stand with your right leg slightly in front of your left, like this."

Robbie copied Josh.

"You don't want to stand up perfectly straight," I said. "Yesterday my sensei said I should bend my knees a bit and get a little lower, so I feel like a sturdy tree with roots going deep into the ground that cannot be knocked over."

Josh smiled at me, and Robbie bent his knees and moved his feet a little farther apart.

"Now, when you punch," said Josh, "you want to make sure that you hit with your first two knuckles, and you want to pull the fist that isn't punching back to your waist. Watch me." Josh did a forward punch. "Now watch Freddy do one."

I did a forward punch.

"You want to make sure you have power in your punch. Pulling that other fist back to your waist at the same time you extend your front arm helps make your punch stronger," said Josh.

Robbie tried one.

"Good!" said Josh. "Try another one."

Robbie did about ten more punches. "Now can you guys show me one of the really cool kicks the Secret Ninjas do?"

"Let's do a side kick," I said.

"Okay," said Josh. "First, hold your hands up in front of your face like this."

Robbie made two fists.

"If you're punching you make fists," said Josh, "but when you're kicking you want to keep your hands open."

"Gotcha!" said Robbie, and he opened his hands.

"The side kick has four parts. You bring your knee up, extend your leg, bring it back in, and then put it down. Like this, one, two, three, four," Josh said as he did the kick really slowly for Robbie. "Now you try it."

Robbie tried, but just like me, his leg wiggled around a little bit.

"That was good," said Josh. "Try again. Hold your left leg steady for balance. One, two, three, four."

Robbie tried again, lost his balance, fell on the ground, and burst out laughing. "This is harder than it looks."

Then came the voice I would know anywhere. "What's so funny, you little wimpy babies?"

How did he find us? I thought to myself.

"Just get out of here," said Josh.

"No, I have some business to take care of with Freddy," said Max.

Josh took a step toward Max, but Max pushed him out of the way and reached to grab me by the collar of my shirt.

Without even thinking, I stuck my right arm up to block his grab and with my left hand, I took hold of his arm. I was eyeball to eyeball and nose to nose with Max Sellars, the biggest bully in the whole second grade.

My stomach flip-flopped. *What have I done?* I thought to myself.

Max just stood there, frozen.

I squeezed Max's arm a little bit tighter. "Get out of here," I whispered in his ear. "Leave us alone!"

My heart was pounding so hard I thought it was going to leap out of my chest, but I didn't

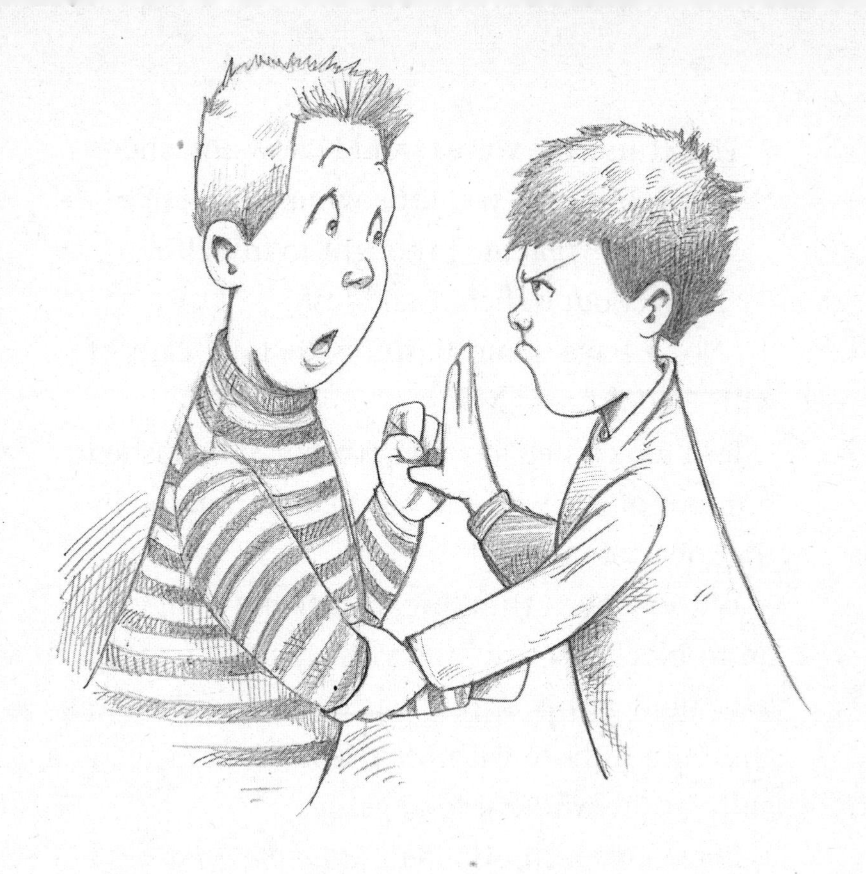

move. Karate had given me the guts to stand up to Max Sellars!

Finally, Max blinked. Then he yanked his arm out of my grasp and took a step backward. I thought he was going to punch me right then and there, but he didn't. He turned around and walked away.

I breathed a big sigh of relief. Whew!

Robbie, Josh, and I all high-fived each other.

"You did it! You did it!" said Josh. "You stood up to Max Sellars!"

"That was awesome!" said Robbie.

I smiled. "Yes, it was," I said. "Yes, it was."

Freddy's Fun Pages

COUNT TO TEN IN JAPANESE

Karate is a martial art that comes from Japan. In karate class, Freddy had to practice his kicks ten times! Learn how to count to ten in Japanese.

One: *ichi* **(ee-chee)**
Two: *ni* **(knee)**
Three: *san* **(sahn)**
Four: *shi* **(she)**
Five: *go* **(go)**
Six: *roku* **(roh-koo)**
Seven: *shichi* **(she-chee)**
Eight: *hachi* **(ha-tchee)**
Nine: *kyuu* **(kyoow)**
Ten: *juu* **(joo)**

PAPER-BAG NINJA

Make your own paper-bag ninja and spar with your friends!

You will need:

A brown lunch bag
Black construction paper
Two googly eyes
Four small metal paper fasteners
Glue
Scissors
Hole punch

Directions:

1. Cut three inches off the bottom of your paper bag to make your ninja the right height.

2. Cut a large rectangle out of the black paper and glue it on the front of the paper bag. (It should cover the entire front of the bag excluding the top flap.)

3. Cut 2 one-inch-wide strips out of the black paper that measure the length of the flap. Glue them on the front flap, making sure to leave space between the two strips for the eyes.

4. Glue the two googly eyes in the empty space on the face between the two black strips.

5. To make the arms and the legs, cut 4 one-inch-wide strips the length you want.

6. To attach the arms, use the hole punch to make one hole at the end of each arm and one hole on each side of the paper bag and attach using the metal paper fasteners.

7. To attach the legs, use the hole punch to make one hole at the end of each leg and two holes at the bottom of the bag and attach using the metal fasteners.

8. Put your hand inside your puppet to play! Remember—you can always position the arms and legs any way you want to make your ninja kick, punch, or block!

ORIGAMI DOG

Origami is the ancient Japanese art of paper folding. Learn how to make this simple origami dog.

Directions:

1. Cut a piece of paper into a 6" x 6" square. You can use any color paper you like.

2. Lay the paper down on a table so it is positioned like a diamond.

3. Fold the top corner down to the bottom corner. You now have a triangle with a straight edge at the top and a point at the bottom.

4. Fold the two top corners down to make ears.

5. Fold only the top layer of the bottom point up a little bit.

6. Fold that layer up again just a little bit to make the nose.

7. Draw eyes and a nose on your dog.

8. You can also draw a tongue on the bottom piece you did not fold up.

Now you can teach your friends!